This Walker book belongs to:

_____

For Anna
Lindsay Camp

For Mum and in loving memory of her little sister, Penny xxx
Lucy Chesher

First published 2012 by Walker Books Ltd, 87 Vauxhall Walk, London SE11 5HJ

This edition published 2013

2 4 6 8 10 9 7 5 3 1

Text © 2012 LNAC Ltd   Illustrations © 2012 Absolutely Cuckoo Ltd

The right of Lindsay Camp and Lucy Chesher to be identified as author and illustrator respectively of
this work has been asserted by them in accordance with the Copyright, Designs and Patents Act 1988

This book has been typeset in Godlike

Printed in China

British Library Cataloguing in Publication Data:a catalogue record for this book is available from the British Library

ISBN 978-1-4063-4761-6

www.walker.co.uk

Yig and Yogg
the Happy Cats

Lindsay Camp   Illustrated by Lucy Chesher

WALKER BOOKS
AND SUBSIDIARIES

LONDON · BOSTON · SYDNEY · AUCKLAND

Yig and Yogg are friends.

That's Yig with the **very big** head.

And that's Yogg with the

very, very big head.

Where Yig and Yogg live, the

sun is always shining.

(Except at night, of course.)

And Yig and Yogg are always happy.

Well, **nearly always...**

Not last Wednesday
but the one before,
the sun was shining and Yig
was watering his flowers.
He had to water them a lot
and it was hard work.

So Yig sat down for a little rest.

Just then, Yogg came by.

"What a lovely colour your
flowers are," she said.

"Just like the sun."

"Yes," said Yig.

"That's what I call them."

"Sunflowers?" said Yogg.

"No," said Yig.

"Just-like flowers."

"Well, I think they're beautiful
just-like flowers," said Yogg.

"Mm, yes," said Yig.
But he sounded a bit worried.

"What's the matter?" said Yogg.
"Well," said Yig, "the thing is,
every time I water my flowers,
I get a bit shorter."

"Do you?" said Yogg.

"Look," said Yig. "Today, I'm just a bit shorter than the tallest flower. But yesterday I was just a bit taller."

"Are you standing up straight?" said Yogg.

"Yes," said Yig. "So I think watering the just-like flowers must be making me shorter."

Yogg laughed. "You are silly, Yig. There are lots of things that could be making you shorter."

"What kind of things?" asked Yig.

"Going to
bed late,"
said Yogg.

"Eating too much peanut butter."

"Wearing the wrong kind of trousers."

"But I haven't been doing any
of those things," said Yig.

"So it must be watering the flowers
that's making me shorter."

"I suppose it could be," said Yogg.

"But I know how we can find out."

"Do you?" said Yig. "You are clever, Yogg!"

"It's easy," said Yogg. "All you have to
do is stop watering the flowers for a
few days. Then we'll be able to see if
you stop getting shorter."

So that's what
Yig did.

He didn't water the
flowers the next day ...

or the day
after that ...

or the day

after that.

"Has it worked?" said Yogg.

"Have you stopped getting shorter?"

"I'm not sure," said Yig. "I don't
feel shorter. But I can't tell unless
I'm standing next to the flowers."

So Yig and Yogg went to the place
where the just-like flowers were.

They were looking rather sad and *droopy.*

Yig stood next to them. He was definitely taller than the tallest flower. "I told you watering the flowers was making me get shorter."

"Hmm," said Yogg. "And not watering them has made you get taller. But the flowers aren't so beautiful any more."

Yig looked worried then. He loved the beautiful just-like flowers. And he didn't want to go on getting taller every day. "Oh Yogg, what am I going to do?"

"Don't worry," said Yogg.

"I've had one of my Brilliant Ideas."

"Have you?" said Yig.

"We'll take it in turns to water the

just-like flowers," said Yogg.

"Then, every day, the one whose turn

it is will get a bit shorter, and the

one whose turn it isn't—"

"Will get a bit taller," said Yig, excitedly.

"That's right," said Yogg.

"So we'll both stay

exactly the same size!"